Darling India

Happy 6th B...

Love from A. Kiki xxx

9993   £2.50

Little Grey Rabbit's Washing Day

Alison Uttley

pictures by Margaret Tempest

Collins

William Collins Sons & Co Ltd
London · Glasgow · Sydney · Auckland
Toronto · Johannesburg

First published 1938
© text The Alison Uttley Literary Property Trust 1987
© illustrations The Estate of Margaret Tempest 1987
© this arrangement William Collins Sons & Co Ltd 1987
Third impression 1988
Cover decoration by Fiona Owen
Decorated capital by Mary Cooper
Alison Uttley's original story has been abridged for this book.
Uttley, Alison
Little Grey Rabbit's washing day. —
Rev. ed — (Little Grey Rabbit books)
I. Title   II. Tempest, Margaret
II. Series
823'.912[J]   PZ10.3

ISBN 0-00-194224-7

Typeset by Columns of Reading
Made and printed in Great Britain by
William Collins Sons and Co Ltd, Glasgow

FOREWORD

Of course you must understand that Grey Rabbit's home had no electric light or gas, and even the candles were made from pith of rushes dipped in wax from the wild bees' nests, which Squirrel found. Water there was in plenty, but it did not come from a tap. It flowed from a spring outside, which rose up from the ground and went to a brook. Grey Rabbit cooked on a fire, but it was a wood fire, there was no coal in that part of the country. Tea did not come from India, but from a little herb known very well to country people, who once dried it and used it in their cottage homes. Bread was baked from wheat ears, ground fine, and Hare and Grey Rabbit gleaned in the cornfields to get the wheat.

The doormats were plaited rushes, like country-made mats, and cushions were stuffed with wool gathered from the hedges where sheep pushed through the thorns. As for the looking-glass, Grey Rabbit found the glass, dropped from a lady's handbag, and Mole made a frame for it. Usually the animals gazed at themselves in the still pools as so many country children have done. The country ways of Grey Rabbit were the country ways known to the author.

I t was a lovely April morning and the sky was blue as a speedwell flower. A fresh wind caught the hazel trees and fluttered their catkins.

Grey Rabbit stood at the window. The curtains flapped against her face and the trees nodded their heads to her.

"Good morning trees," said she. "I hope you are well." But the trees didn't answer. They only tossed their branches and shook their thousand yellow tails, so that the golden pollen flew in a shower.

There was a thump and a bump and Hare came bounding into the room.

"Grey Rabbit," he called. "What are you staring at?"

"The nut trees waving in the wind," said Grey Rabbit.

"Is breakfast ready?" said Squirrel, dancing in.

Just then, they heard the sound of singing in the lane.

They could hear the words clearly.

> "The gipsy walks the long road,
> Her basket on her head.
> Her house is in the woodland,
> The bracken is her bed."

There was a click of the garden gate. Somebody was coming up the path. It was a gipsy rabbit, with a green rush basket perched on her head. Round her neck was a coloured shawl. She was very brown, and her hair was rough and tousled. She came up to the door singing her song:

> "Come buy my shining clothes-pegs,
> With bands of silver bound,
> And peg your little apron
> In orchard drying-ground."

The gipsy put her basket on the door-step and nodded and smiled.

"Kind Grey Rabbit," said she, "You'll buy my clothes-pegs, won't you?"

She stooped to the basket, and held up the neat roll of wooden pegs, with little silver bands round their waists. They were threaded together like a row of small dolls.

"Oh, how lovely!" cried Grey Rabbit. "I've always wanted some clothes-pegs to keep my washing from blowing away. Will these clothes-pegs keep the things fast on the line?" she asked.

"Yes, indeed, Grey Rabbit," said the gipsy. "I've sold my little pegs to many families all over the world, and I have had many a letter thanking me."

She dived in her pocket and brought out a bundle of leaves. Even as she sorted them a gust of wind seized them and tossed them away.

"Oh dear!" cried Grey Rabbit. "All your letters gone."

"Plenty more," said the gipsy calmly. "Plenty more where these came from."

"It would be nice to have some real clothes-pegs," mused Grey Rabbit, and Squirrel and Hare nodded.

"These clothes-pegs will keep your washing on the line when the wind blows, Grey Rabbit. You need never fear it will go," said the gipsy.

"Then I will buy them," said Grey Rabbit, and she clapped her paws for joy.

Squirrel was leaning over the gipsy's basket
on the ground.

"Here's a brush to brush my tail," said she.
"I should like this. And here's a tin
saucepan," she added.

"We've got a saucepan," said Hare. "Don't
be silly, Squirrel."

The gipsy smiled at Squirrel, and the little
animal dived with her paws under the shining
objects which filled the basket.

"Here's something," she said, "What is it
for? I'm sure we want it."

"It's a nutmeg grater," said the gipsy. "And
here's the little box to keep the nutmeg in."

"Oh! What is inside? A nut?" squeaked
Squirrel.

"A nutmeg," said the gipsy. "It comes from over the sea. It doesn't grow in our woods."

They passed the nutmeg from one to another, and smelled it and licked it.

"What's it for?" asked Grey Rabbit.

"You rub it on the grater, and sprinkle it in your cakes," said the gipsy.

"Oh, do buy the nutmeg grater, Grey Rabbit," shouted Hare, and Grey Rabbit agreed.

Then the gipsy sang another verse of her song:

> "I bought the wooden clothes-pegs,
> With their girdles of new tin,
> I bought a little grater,
> To keep my nutmeg in."

Grey Rabbit put her hand in her pocket and brought out an empty purse. She ran into the house and looked in the money box. There was nothing in it. She peeped in the teapot and in the clock. There was nothing at all.

"Oh dear!" she sighed. "What shall I do? I would like to have those clothes-pegs."

"Oh dear!" echoed Squirrel. "I do want the nutmeg grater."

The gipsy looked at them with dark flashing eyes, and sang again:

> "I hadn't any money,
> But the gipsy didn't care,
> 'Just a pair of ear-rings,
> I'll take for them, my dear.'"

"Ear-rings!" cried Grey Rabbit and Squirrel.

Grey Rabbit whispered to Squirrel and Squirrel ran up the hazel tree. She picked two little clusters of hazel catkins with their long greeny-yellow tails.

"Will these do?" asked Grey Rabbit, offering them to the gipsy.

"Just right," said the gipsy, and she fastened them to her ears, and let them dangle like a pair of pretty tassels.

"Thank you Grey Rabbit. Thank you Squirrel and Hare," said the gipsy. "Good luck to your wash-day."

"Thank you. Good luck to you," they called.

Then away went the gipsy with her skirt flapping and her ear-rings bobbing and her dark eyes sparkling.

Down the lane she went. They could hear her song, shrill and clear, like a blackbird's whistle.

"Listen!" cried Hare, and this is what they heard:

> "I washed my little apron
> And hung it up to dry.
> The gipsy waved her hand to me,
> And vanished in the sky."

They stood for a while looking up into the sky, but nowhere could they see the gipsy rabbit. Then they returned to the house with their treasures.

Grey Rabbit was longing to use her new, bright clothes-pegs. She thought they should have a wash-day. The sun was shining and the little wind would dry the clothes. She sent Hare across the common to ask if anybody wanted any clothes washed.

Hare nodded importantly and galloped off. He knocked at every little cottage in the woods and lanes.

"Any washing today? Grey Rabbit's wash-day."

Out came the little animals with small garments, cobweb scarves, tiny handker-chiefs, leafy towels. Some put their clothes in wheelbarrows. Some scampered with trailing sheets. And Hare ran on, calling: "Any washing today for Grey Rabbit?"

He even went to Wise Owl and rang the bell.
Wise Owl woke up and opened the door a
crack.

"Go away! I don't want anything," he said,
when he saw Hare. "Go away. I'm asleep."
He shook his head violently and his nightcap
fell off and floated down to Hare.

"Thank you, Sir," said Hare.

Mrs Hedgehog said that Fuzzypeg's smock
was dirty, and she would be very glad if Grey
Rabbit would wash it.

Moldy Warp asked Hare if Grey Rabbit
would wash his best scarf.

The Speckledy Hen sent her green sun-
bonnet, and Mrs Rat gave Hare her apron.

Everybody was glad little Grey Rabbit was
going to have a real wash-day and there was a
scutter of little feet bearing garments for the
wash-tub.

Grey Rabbit put her own handkerchiefs
and nightgown and blue apron in the wash,
and Squirrel brought her yellow dress.

Hare warmed the water and carried it
outside and poured it in a tub. Everything was
ready but there was no soap. High and low
they hunted, under the table, in the wood-
shed. At last Grey Rabbit found it in the
flour-bin, where Hare had left it on baking
day.

Squirrel ran up the apple tree and tied the
clothes-line to a branch. Then she ran up the
pear tree and fastened the other end.

Grey Rabbit stood at the wash-tub which Hare had placed among the daisies. She rubbed and scrubbed and dipped each little garment, and soaped and rinsed them till they were clean. Then she tossed them into the clothes-basket, and Hare and Squirrel carried them to the stream. They dabbled them in the clear water, shook them, and threw them up in the air like balls.

"Now to hang them on the line," said Grey Rabbit, when they returned, laughing and swinging the basket. "Now for the little clothes-pegs."

She climbed on an upturned tub and pegged each article, as Squirrel held it to her.

The wind came hurrying over the grass, and it tugged and pulled at the little garments, but the shining gipsy clothes-pegs held them firmly. So it blew into each one and puffed it out as if it were alive. The clothes leaped and danced on the line; the little smocks filled out as if small fat bodies were inside them; the furry stockings looked as if they had a pair of legs.

The clothes-pegs held tightly to the line, the silver bands glittered, the rope swung, and all the clothes bobbed and curtsied.

Now somebody else was watching the row of washing dancing on the clothes-line. It was the Fox. He thought it was a party. He saw Fuzzypeg's smock and Squirrel's yellow dress, all puffed out, and he licked his lips.

"Fuzzypeg and Squirrel having a swing," said he. "Lots of people swinging! They look uncommonly fat! If I creep up very quietly, I may catch them and carry them home for tea."

He crept up very softly and took a great spring.

Whoo-oo-oo! whistled the wind.

Swish-swish! went the clothes-line.

Tinkle! Tinkle! rang the little clothes-pegs and the Fox leapt back in alarm.

"Dear me!" he cried. "There's nobody inside them. They are only wind-bags!"

And away he went, feeling very cross.

Next came a weasel. He was passing, looking for something to eat, and he saw the row of washing, bobbing and dancing on the line.

"Hullo! Fat little animals swinging on a rope. Just right for my tea!" said he. "I'll grab that stout little fellow in the blue smock."

He took a hop and a leap right over the garden bed, and he sprang on the back of Fuzzypeg's wind-filled smock. But he clasped nothing at all!

Whoo-oo-oo! whistled the wind.

Swish-sh-sh, hissed the clothes-line.

Tinkle-tinkle, rang the little clothes-pegs, and the weasel fell on the ground with a thump.

"Nothing in them. Empty clothes," he muttered. And off he went.

Next came Old Hedgehog with his cans of milk. "Hullo! What's young Fuzzypeg doing here, a-swinging on Grey Rabbit's clothes-line?"

He crept softly up to the clothes-line and grabbed the smock. Tinkle-tinkle rang the little clothes-pegs.

"Dear me! It isn't Fuzzypeg at all! It's only his smock filled with air."

Grey Rabbit came running from the house with Squirrel and Hare close behind. "Oh Hedgehog! Did you hear some bells ringing?"

"Yes, Miss Grey Rabbit. Bells ring if you touch the washing-line. Where ever did you get such wonderful pegs?" said Old Hedgehog.

"I bought them from a gipsy," said Grey Rabbit.

"Ah! There's been a gipsy sleeping in the bracken. Yes, I saw her, but when I turned round she had gone!"

Grey Rabbit took down the dry clothes and Hare and Squirrel folded them and laid them in a basket.

"I got a nutmeg grater from the gipsy," said Squirrel. "Have you ever seen a nutmeg, Hedgehog?"

"Can't say as I have," said Hedgehog.

"Here it is," said Squirrel, bringing it from her pocket.

Hedgehog examined it, and smelled it.

"If you use it, it will be gone, and there's an end of it. If you plant it, you'll maybe get a nutmeg tree," said he.

"I'm going to plant it now," said Hare. He dug a little hole and pushed the nutmeg into the ground. Then he helped Squirrel to carry the washing back to the house.

"My missis will come and help with the ironing," said Hedgehog. "She's a champion ironer."

So Mrs Hedgehog came to iron the little garments. She brought with her a small flat iron. Fuzzypeg sat watching his mother, and Grey Rabbit hung the things round the fire to air.

When the work was finished Hare and Fuzzypeg carried the piles of little garments back to the woods and commons. But of course Hare forgot where many of the things belonged.

He dropped little handkerchiefs and mufflers and scarves and collars in every hole and doorway he could find. The mice and the dormice, the spider and the fly, the rabbits and squirrels, all got the wrong clothes.

He hung Mole's purple scarf on a holly tree and Moldy Warp had to get a ladder to reach it. He tied Wise Owl's nightcap to the bell-rope of the beech tree where Wise Owl lived.

All the little clothes were sprinkled about the fields, on bluebells and dandelions and primroses.

"Did you deliver the washing, Hare?" asked Grey Rabbit.

"I got rid of it, Grey Rabbit," said Hare. "They will all find their clothes if they look."

"Oh, Hare!" Grey Rabbit shook her head.

When Grey Rabbit lay in bed that night she heard a sound of singing in the lane. She ran to the window and leaned out.

Along the path came the gipsy rabbit. She glided past the garden wall and her song came to Grey Rabbit's quick ears, although it was soft as a whisper.

"Too-whit, too-whoo!" hooted Wise Owl in the wood and the gipsy was silent. Grey Rabbit crept back to bed.

But the next day – there was a little nutmeg tree growing in the garden! It was covered with pink flowers and green leaves. When Hare ran out to look at it he found some brown nutmegs growing in the branches.

"A real gipsy, full of magic," said he, and Grey Rabbit and Squirrel agreed.

"The gipsy walks the long road,
Her basket on her head.
Her house is in the woodland,
The bracken is her bed.

"I bought some little clothes-pegs,
With magic bells a-ringing.
I pegged my little apron,
And the clothes began a-singing.

"I bought a little nutmeg,
And set it in the ground.
A fine flowery nutmeg tree,
Came springing from the mound."